Jungle Tails

Adventures with Three Animal Friends

written by Wendy Wax

illustrated by Michael Terry

Reader's Digest
Children's Books®

Pleasantville, New York • Montréal, Québec • Bath, United Kingdom

What Zebra Likes

I am Zebra. Do you know what I like best about the jungle? My friends!

When I go to play with them, I like to do all the things they like to do.

When I'm with Hippopotamus, we float in the water with just our eyes and noses peeking out.

What do the fish think when they see my stripy self underwater? Do they mistake me for a hippo?

When I'm with Leopard, we lounge around on shady branches. Down below, animals pass by, but nobody sees us. What would they say if they knew that a leopard and a zebra were spying on them from above?

I like swinging from vines with Monkey, though I am still perfecting my technique.

I like slithering through the grass with Snake, though my legs sometimes get in the way.

And I like standing on one leg with
Flamingo—at least, I *try* to stand on one leg.

But when my friends come to play with me, we get to do the things I like best. That's when I have the most fun of all.

Hippo Rules

I am Hippopotamus—but you can call me King of the River.

"Who made you King?" croaks Frog.

"I did," I say. "I'm the biggest animal around. So you'd better treat me with respect...or else!"

Here comes Leopard. There goes Leopard.
He didn't even bother to say hello—so I
splash him. "Next time treat me with respect!"
I shout.

Then Zebra passes by. She is noisy—so I snap at her. "The King of the River needs peace and quiet," I shout.

"Who made you King?" asks Zebra. Then she trots away.

Now it is quiet—too quiet. Where is everyone? There they are—at the watering hole!

"Hey, there!" I call, but no one hears me. They are too busy having fun. They are all friends.

I am not having fun. I have no friends, but I wish I did.

I know! I will tell them they have to be my friends. After all, I am King of the River.

When I get to the watering hole, everyone stops talking.

"Be my friends!" I demand.

"No," says Zebra. "Friends don't snap at each other."

"No," says Leopard. "Friends don't splash each other."

"No," says Frog. "Friends don't boss each other around."

"Then what do friends do?" I ask.

"Friends are nice to each other. They treat each other with respect," says Leopard.

"I think I can do that," I say.

Guess what! I have friends now. I am nice to them, and they are nice to me. I respect them, and they respect me. Having friends is fun!

Oh…by the way, don't call me King of the River. Being King was no fun at all. Just call me Hippo, and maybe we can be friends, too.

Where Is Leopard?

I'm speedy! I'm sneaky! I'm Leopard! And I'm about to play hide-and-seek with my friends.

"I hide. You seek," I say.

"I want to hide," says Hippopotamus. But by then I've disappeared!

"Ready or not, here we come!" my friends shout.

I go for a swim at the watering hole. They will never look for me here. They know leopards don't need much water, and that most cats don't swim. (But I do!)

Uh-oh! I was wrong! Here they come!

I slip underwater, glide to the far bank, and race into the forest.

I'm speedy! I'm sneaky! I'm having fun!

All afternoon, I hide from my friends. I can see them, but they can't see me.

When Zebra sees my shadow, it quickly disappears. When Hippopotamus sees my footprints, they lead to the foot of the tree I'm in—so I leap to a different tree.

When my friends are here, I am there. When they are there, I am here. I am everywhere they're not. They are nowhere I am.

I'm speedy! I'm sneaky! And I'm... getting tired.

"I give up," says Zebra, as the sun sets.

"Me, too," says Hippopotamus. "Leopard is too fast and sneaky for me."

Zzzzzzzzzz. Zzzzzzzzzz.

Who is snoring?

Zebra and Hippo follow the snores, and guess who they find....

Me!

Hippopotamus yawns.

Zebra yawns.

This has been a long day.

"Let's play hide-and-seek again tomorrow," says Zebra.

Hippopotamus agrees. "But tomorrow it's our turn to hide."